Th... End
of the Rainbow

To

Winnie

" Enjoy Reading "

Lorraine Hellier

Lorraine Hellier

The Other End of the Rainbow

Matador
9 De Montfort Mews
Leicester LE1 7FW, UK
Tel: (+44) 116 255 9311 / 9312
Email: books@troubador.co.uk
Web: www.troubador.co.uk/matador

ISBN 10: 1-905886-23-3
ISBN 13: 978-1-905886-23-4

Cover illustrations © Steve Harper

Typeset in 14pt Bembo by Troubador Publishing Ltd, Leicester, UK
Printed in the UK by The Cromwell Press Ltd, Trowbridge, Wilts, UK

Matador is an imprint of Troubador Publishing Ltd

For my Dad

Contents

Chapter 1

The Antique Shop

"Part time assistant required
suit young person
apply within"

The notice on the door had caught Zoë's attention as she passed every day on her way to school. The postcard was written in red ink. Today she'd made a decision.

Had she the courage to go in? She walked past the shop and stopped at the corner of the street. All of these shops were dark and gloomy. She couldn't understand why she felt drawn like a magnet to this one. Buttoning up her winter coat, she tried to hide her school uniform, winding a bright red scarf around her neck to cover the school tie. Then she turned and walked back. She reached out her hand and pushed open the door.

As Zoë entered, a tiny bell rang. She carefully stepped around several small tables which displayed various ornaments, clocks, vases and other small items for sale. There was hardly room to move, as there was such an abundance of surplus stock in the dark interior of the shop.

She glanced around the walls at the oil paintings in old-fashioned frames, and ornate mirrors with tarnished glass.

From the back of the shop a small, elderly man appeared. His hair and beard were almost snow white, his bright blue eyes inquisitive.

She wandered towards him.

'Can I help you, Miss?'

She hesitated slightly, looking behind, then back at the old gentleman. 'I was wondering about the job. Do you have to have experience?'

'Well, not really. Were you interested?'

She looked down at her feet, noticing how muddy her shoes were. She lifted her head and taking a deep breath, trying to steady her nerves, she saw he was waiting for her to reply.

'Yes, I'm looking for a part time job on Saturdays and …'

She paused, wondering if to continue, then deciding to be honest, she added: 'And after school, to earn some pocket money for a school trip to Italy.'

'Sounds ideal. I need a bit of help, you can probably tell from the clutter.' He grinned as he waved his hand around the overcrowded room. 'Saturday morning and a few hours in the week to tidy up and help in the shop.'

'That would be great. How do I apply?'

The old man sat down on a rather shabby looking dining chair. 'How about we forget the formalities, give each other a trial, and see how we get on for a month. Then if we're both happy, we can make it official.'

Zoë smiled and heaved a sigh of relief, as he asked:'What's your name?'

'Zoë Chappell.' Zoë wanted to give a good impression, so she stretched out her hand politely. He took her hand and squeezed it gently.

'Well, Zoë. I'm Phineas. Can you come this Saturday?'

Zoë was thrilled. She was fascinated by the bits and bobs, and she looked forward to rummaging through the stock.

She nodded and grinned back. 'What time?' she asked.

'Oh, say about nine, is that O.K?'

'Fine, see you Saturday then.'

Zoë left the shop, mentally rearranging the tables, wondering how she could persuade her new employer to allow her to do a window display to attract customers. She was sure she could be an asset to the little antique shop.

★

When Zoë arrived home her mother called out: 'You're late Zoë. Where have you been?'

Zoë slung her school bag in the corner of the hall and threw her coat over the banister.

'I've got myself a part-time job, Mum.' She bounced into the kitchen. 'What's for tea?'

She opened the fridge and took out a carton of orange juice. Her mother passed her a glass from the cupboard above her head.

'Spaghetti Bolognese. Your Dad's working late again.'

'Oh. Surprise, surprise...' Zoë said sarcastically.

'How was school today?'

'It's horrible. I hate it here. I don't like being "the new girl." I miss my old friends. The girls already have their own friends here and they don't include me in anything... and the teachers pick on me.'

'I'm sure they don't, Zoë. It will get better, it just takes time.'

Zoë sat down at the kitchen table. 'Anyway, this little job will give me something to do.'

'You didn't tell me you were going after a job.'

'I was on the way back from school and I saw the notice in the shop window in Old Market Street.'

'Which one? I don't remember any shops down there that would take on a teenager. They're mostly estate agents, solicitors and banks.'

'It's that little antique shop. The old man wants a bit of help. Saturday morning and a couple of hours after school.'

'You mean at the end of the terrace, that dusty, shabby place?'

'Yes, Mum. That's why he needs help, cleaning and sorting the stock.'

'I'd better come and meet this old man before you agree to work there.'

'Oh, Mum. Do you have to? You'll embarrass me.'

Her mother continued stirring the Bolognese. 'Zoë … in this day and age, sadly we have to be sure of your safety.'

She had no choice but to agree that her mother came with her on Saturday morning and meet her future employer.

Zoë had no idea that this was only the beginning of an adventure.

Chapter 2

Phineas

On Saturday morning Zoë was up early. She dressed in jeans and T-shirt and her favourite denim jacket. She clipped back her dark hair with two hair slides, put on her trainers and called to her mum:

'I'm going now, if you really want to check out the old man…'

Zoë turned from her mother making frustrated gestures of annoyance at her mother still insisting on coming with her.

At five minutes to nine they stood outside the shop. Zoë cupped her hands round her eyes, peering through the cloudy window, but could not see the proprietor. Various plates, jugs and basins, ornaments and mirrors were piled in front of the window. Everything looked dusty. At nine o'clock sharp, the old man appeared inside the shop. He opened up and they followed him inside.

'Morning, Phineas. This is my mother, she wanted to meet you.'

Phineas held out his hand. 'Nice to meet you, Mrs. Chappell. Is there a problem?'

Zoë watched her mother closely, hoping she wouldn't embarrass her.

'Not at all. I just wanted to show an interest in Zoë working here, and meet her employer.'

Phineas turned to Zoë. She wasn't sure if she detected a note of sarcasm in his voice.

'How sensible of your mother to check me out.'

Phineas led them into the shop and stood by a large antique desk. 'For today I thought we could go around the shop and make some plans of what you can do. If you can come on Saturday mornings and a couple of hours after school one day a week, we should soon see some improvement. What do you think, Zoë?'

Zoë joined her thumb and forefinger into a circle in an expression of perfection. Her mother agreed and then left the shop.

'Mothers can be overprotective,' Phineas sympathised, patting Zoë's arm.

He picked up a notepad and pen from the table in front of him. They weaved their way between the antique furniture as he led the way to the back of the shop. He showed her a hidden opening to a tiny room. It was like a small kitchen. There was a table and two chairs, a sink, kettle and mugs. From this room was a steep staircase.

'Shall I put the kettle on? We could have a drink while we chat.'

Phineas grinned and replied. 'I think I'm going to be pleased I've taken you on, Zoë.'

They sat drinking their tea and talking about how the shop could be made more appealing for customers. Phineas admitted it needed a good clean.

'I'm a bit worried about knocking things off those little tables, Phineas.'

As he looked to see where Zoë was pointing, he nodded: 'Yes, it is a bit difficult to get round safely. It's a wonder my customers haven't broken anything before, isn't it?'

'We could put some away, couldn't we?'

'Yes, I think you're right, Zoë. You could pick some nice pieces to put in the window and we'll have a good tidy up.'

Phineas showed Zoë around the antiques. The items were tagged with a short description and price. Some of the labels were torn and had faded.

'That's one little job that you could do for

me, Zoë, replace the tags with nice new ones.'

Zoë's morning went quickly. She told him about her school trip and how she was looking forward to going to Italy. Somehow she couldn't help feeling there was something mysterious about Phineas. She had a feeling of excitement and anticipation, like looking forward to Christmas or a holiday, yet she couldn't understand why.

★

On Thursday after school Zoë changed out of her school uniform and reminded her mother she was working at the antique shop. She arrived just after four o'clock. Phineas greeted her with a huge grin.

'You came then. I haven't lost you yet?'

She took off her jacket, tied her hair back with a scrunchie and started running hot water into a bucket.

'What are you doing, Zoë?'

She turned around, blushing. 'Oh, I'm sorry Phineas, I should have asked first. Is it OK if I clean the windows? They're so dusty.'

Phineas laughed, his hands flew up and waved about. 'Zoë you're priceless. I think we're going to be great friends. Go ahead. I can't complain about your willingness to get stuck in.'

First, she took the bucket of water, then a chair from the kitchen outside and cleaned the windows and the frames. She started on the inside of the shop window, carefully moving the stock away. The glass was soon clear and she was pleased with herself. It had made such an improvement. She selected a few items to display and put the rest in a cardboard box she'd found under the kitchen table.

She stood back admiring the window. She wanted Phineas to see. Wondering where he'd gone, she went into the little back room and started up the stairs. This was the only place he could be. She called his name, but there was no reply.

At the top of the stairs there was nothing, except a grandfather clock. It had a sun and moon decorative inset and a gold face. The time on the clock was ten past five. The front panel was slightly open.

Zoë called out again. 'Phineas are you up here?'

She was puzzled because there were no other doors. The only piece of furniture was the clock. There were no windows, so it was quite dim. She heard Phineas's voice.

'Come through, Zoë'

'Come through where?'

'Through the clock, it is open.'

Zoë opened the panel fully and saw daylight beyond.

Chapter 3

Serendipity

Zoë stepped into the clock. Phineas sat on a bench at the edge of a lake.

Zoë's eyes widened. She didn't know what to say or do. Should she turn back? She looked around her. How could she after seeing this vision? Her curiosity, and the beauty of this place, would not let her go. She was mesmerized. She had to find out more about this amazing place.

Phineas patted the bench indicating she should join him.

'Where are we, Phineas?' she whispered.

'This is Lake Tanamere. Across there, the island is Serendipity, my home. Perhaps you'd like to visit?'

The island was about half a mile from the pier where they sat.

'I'd love to, but I have to get home, my

Mum gives me an ear bashing if I'm late.' Zoë sighed. She was disappointed. She felt as if she'd been deprived of a special treat.

'Time stands still here, Zoë. We're in a different dimension. No matter what time you go back through the clock, you'll return at just the same time you entered it.'

A few yards from where they sat were two black swans with red beaks. Droplets of water glistened on their feathers in the sunlight. There were several small boats tied to the deck, shaped like large nutshells.

Zoë looked across the lake to the island. It appeared to be in a huge bubble. Above it was a rainbow, the whole spectrum shining vividly. She was used to seeing faint insipid colours. The arc dipped down into the bubble, as if the end finished inside it. Phineas took Zoë's hand and led her to one of the boats. It was shaped like a large Brazil nutshell.

'I'll take you across to my home on Serendipity. You can see my house.' Phineas helped Zoë into the boat and picked up the oars.

As he rowed across the short distance to the island, Zoë's mind was full of questions but she didn't know where to begin. She saw ahead this beautiful vision of colours, sparkling in the sunlight. She could think of nothing to compare it with or describe the feelings it stirred in her. There was a sense of beauty and tranquillity. It filled her with emotions she'd never experienced before.

Zoë could see through the bubble that the island had thick woods of tall pine trees. She could hear the rushing water of a river. The twittering of various birds filled the air. The fresh smell of country air mixed with the tangy smell of the sea.

She leaned out of the boat and dipped her fingers in the water. It was warm, which surprised her. As she caught Phineas watching her, she grinned.

Phineas stopped rowing. 'You're very quiet. You do want to come Zoë, don't you?'

'Oh, Phineas. Yes. I'm just so overcome. It takes my breath away.'

'That's partly why it has to be protected. There are those, who would like to spoil the calmness and serenity, and steal the secrets of Serendipity.'

Phineas took, from his pocket, an unusual shaped piece of glass. It was long and narrow, with several sides which reflected the light. Phineas explained that the rod-like glass was a sort of key.

'It's like a prism, it refracts the light from the sun.'

He gently pushed the prism into the bubble. The area in front of them dissolved to form a gateway for them to enter the bubble into a small cave. They stepped out of the boat and walked a few yards through a copse into a clearing.

There ahead of them was a derelict house. It looked empty. Zoë would not have imagined this was where Phineas lived. The wood looked scorched as if there had been a fire at some time. The roof needed re-thatching. The guttering was hanging off the wall. The window shutters were broken and swinging loose on their hinges. It was like something due for demolition. She could even imagine a bulldozer appearing from behind the house.

She didn't want to offend Phineas, but her heart sank and it must have shown in her face, because Phineas wagged his finger at her, saying: 'Remember that saying: appearances can be deceptive? Well, this is the best example you'll ever see. The island is called Serendipity, which means: making of pleasant discoveries. This is one such deception for you to discover.'

Chapter 4

Phineas' House

He opened the door. The dusty interior did nothing to lift Zoë's spirit. She followed Phineas through an open door, only to gasp as he stood to the side, letting her see the interior of the room. As her eyes wandered around she saw that Phineas was not exaggerating. In front of her was a sitting room, with a large picture window, directly opposite, looking out over a beautiful garden.

The window frame was draped with soft cream-coloured muslin, gracefully looped at the top and sides through hoops made of mother of pearl. As Zoë and Phineas stepped into the room, their feet were cushioned by a soft, velvety carpet, which had a sheen to it. It gave the illusion of shimmering sand.

'This is really cool.' Zoë spun around to Phineas. He smiled.

The room gave an aura of peace the moment she stepped into it. The sofas and chairs were covered with an oyster-coloured silk, with scatter cushions of palest pinks and peach. Zoë sat down on the nearest sofa. She picked up a fluffy pink cushion and hugged it.

'Phineas, it's…beautiful! I don't know what to say.' She gazed around the room. There were several pictures on the walls. They were painted in pastel shades, some of idyllic dream settings, others of various woodland creatures. There were huge ornate mirrors reflecting the room.

Zoë could smell a mixture of aromas, flowers and spices. She shivered. It was slightly cool, but so clean compared to the pollution of the city that Zoë was used to.

Phineas brought over a tray, with two small glasses of a pale rose pink coloured drink, and some star-shaped golden biscuits. Zoë and Phineas sat silently sipping the juice. It was a mixture of fruits from the island. The biscuits melted in the mouth, tasting of ginger and cinnamon and spices she'd never sampled before. Zoë put her drink down on a small glass topped table, the base shaped like a seashell.

Phineas walked over to the window. 'Come and see my beautiful garden, Zoë.'

She went over to join him.

'I'll show you properly when you come again.'

He pointed out the waterfall, and a stream which passed through the garden under a tiny rugged stone bridge.

He went on to explain more about the island: 'The island is home to many creatures, who are free to live in harmony together. The code of life here is that we respect each other. There is much more to learn about Serendipity, but I must warn you, it is a privilege that you have been allowed to visit here. You must not divulge the secrets of the island.'

'I understand what an honour it is for me to come here, Phineas. Thank you so much for bringing me. I will treasure this day forever. I hope I have the chance to come again.'

'You will. Next time maybe you can meet some of my friends.'

They walked away from the window, out of the beautiful sitting room, into the sunlight. Zoë glanced back at the house, as they made their way back to the boat. The house really did hide a secret. Zoë knew that inside was beauty. As Phineas had warned her not to be guided by first impressions, she felt maybe she was being taught a lesson.

Phineas was waiting in the boat. Zoë stepped in, the boat glided across the lake. When they arrived at the other side and stepped back through the clock, Phineas pointed to the time, ten past five. As he'd said, time in this dimension had stood still.

Zoë had been silent on the return journey. Now she turned to Phineas and, with tears in her eyes, flung her arms around him and whispered: 'Thank you, Phineas. Thank you. I'll see you soon.' Phineas smiled.

She ran down the stairs and out of the shop.

Zoë kept her word. Phineas need not worry about sharing Serendipity with her. Although Zoë knew it was not a dream but another world she had visited, she thought it would dissolve like mist if she uttered a word.

She lived for her next visit to the island, wondering who she would meet.

Chapter 5

Another Dimension

On Saturday morning Zoë greeted Phineas with a beaming smile. He didn't mention anything about their last encounter. She soon calmed down and remembered she was here to work.

Her task today was to start dusting and polishing the furniture. She noticed a few items were missing from her window display.

'There have been several sales this week, Zoë. I'm sure it's because you cleaned my shop window and did that window display.'

Zoë chose a lovely golden antique dressing table set comprising of a mirror, comb and a trinket box, to put in the window. She also added a little mantel clock and two matching vases with peacocks painted on them.

'I need to go to the bank across the road, Zoë. Will you be all right on your own for half an hour?'

Zoë shrugged her shoulders and carried on washing the vases.

'You can lock the door if you want to.' Phineas left via the shop door, wearing his coat and an old-fashioned bowler hat, and carrying a carved ebony walking stick.

Zoë felt disappointed that Phineas hadn't mentioned Serendipity. Then she told herself that Phineas had a business to run and couldn't just stop and take her to the island.

As she wandered around, her mind drifted back to her visit. She picked up the mirror from the window display, fingering the filigree design which, although tarnished with age, she'd rather taken to. Turning the mirror over, instead of seeing her reflection, she saw to her amazement, Phineas's house. It had the same derelict appearance as when she'd last seen it. She remembered his words about not being fooled by first impressions. She smiled and placed the mirror back in the window.

Zoë was really pleased this little job was working out. It was quieter than working in a supermarket or fast food take-away.

'Back to work,' she thought. Gently moving chairs and small tables away from the wall, she swept one side of the room. The larger pieces of furniture would be impossible to move, so she dusted and polished them.

Suddenly, she jumped as the shop doorbell buzzed. An elderly lady came in. Zoë watched her as she looked around the shop.

'Are you in charge, young lady?' she asked abruptly.

'Yes. Can I help you?' Zoë tried to sound professional, but really her mouth was dry and she felt very nervous. She wished Phineas would come back.

'The little mantel clock in the window. Does it work?'

'Yes, Madam. My boss always has stock repaired before displaying for customers. Would you like a closer look? I could get it from the window for you.'

The lady touched her grey hair, adjusted the scarf at her neck and nodded affirmative. She was dressed all in black and reminded Zoë of a bird, maybe a crow.

Zoë fetched the clock. Checking a label was attached to it for the price, she placed it on a small table in front of the customer.

Knowing nothing about the little clock, Zoë realised she would have to bluff her way. She put her hands behind her back, suddenly conscious of her bitten fingernails and crossing her fingers on both hands. She started tentatively: 'It's lovely isn't it?'

'Yes. I think it would make an ideal present for my sister's birthday.'

Just then Phineas returned. Zoë breathed a sigh of relief. He nodded at Zoë and left her to carry on.

Without asking any further questions, the old lady decided to buy the clock. She followed Zoë to the counter at the back of the shop. She didn't query the price, just wrote the cheque. Zoë stamped it with the shop stamp: "Another Dimension."

Zoë grinned. What an apt name for the shop. She hadn't realised. There wasn't a name outside.

'What are you grinning at?' Phineas asked as the lady left the shop.

'The name of your shop, it's most appropriate, if anyone knew...' She pointed upwards. 'I was so glad when you came back. I didn't know what to say.'

'You were fine. You've made your first sale. Well done.'

'Thanks Boss.'

She felt proud of herself and smiled at Phineas as he put the cheque away.

'How about a visit to my island? Would you like to go today?'

Zoë nodded enthusiastically.

'Well, I think you deserve it. You lock the shop door and meet me by the lake. I'll wait by the boats.'

Zoë quickly washed her hands, shut up the shop and ran up the stairs. The clock panel was open, it was ten to twelve as she entered, and there was Phineas waiting.

Chapter 6

Roseena

Soon they were crossing the calm, deep lake in the nutshell boat. The sun shone through the bubble, reflecting all the colours of the rainbow above. Phineas used the rod-like key to dissolve the entrance and they drifted through. They walked to the clearing where Phineas' house stood just as Zoë remembered it.

'I think we'll go through to the garden. I'd like you to meet my daughter, Roseena.'

'Sorry, Phineas. I didn't even think of your family. I'd love to meet Roseena. How old is she?'

'Roseena is my only child. She's fourteen. I know I'm biased as her father, but she's a pretty girl and I am very protective of her.'

They approached the house, taking a side gate that opened into the garden. Zoë followed Phineas, breathing in the fragrances of honeysuckle, mimosa and sweet smelling roses. The cool air was fresh from droplets splashing from the waterfall. There were trees of so many varieties, the colours blending as only Nature can portray: willows, Japanese maple, Eucalyptus, magnolia, silver birch and yew trees.

Phineas showed Zoë around the garden.

'What's that lovely sweet smell?'

'That will be the lilac and honeysuckle.' He pointed out the ivy and wisteria climbing the over the boundary walls. Phineas was proud of the garden: 'See there's lily of the valley, roses, fuchsia, Canterbury bells, violets.'

Zoë thought how colourful it was compared to the small patch of gravel, with a few pots of dying specimens of brown dried leaves, which her parents called a garden.

So many different plants here, growing together regardless of weather, time of year or type of soil. In this garden of paradise, with these ideal conditions, everything flourished in harmony.

Zoë saw the water lilies on the pond and asked if there were any fish.

'Sometimes fish come up the stream from other parts of the island. They are free to swim where they want.'

Without a word Phineas walked towards

the waterfall, then suddenly stopped. 'Oh, by the way, you won't get wet as we walk through the waterfall. It's our gateway to the island.' Phineas disappeared through the waterfall.

Zoë followed, hesitantly at first then, discovering she had been holding her breath, she relaxed and quickened her pace to catch up with Phineas.

It was so lovely walking through the waterfall that Zoë felt like she had left all her worries behind. She imagined it being a healing experience of the mind and body, it was like a new beginning.

Phineas was sitting on a tree stump to the left as she came into a clearing. He was playing a small silver flute.

A few yards ahead coming towards them, from a pathway among the trees, was a slight figure. She was exquisite, in a white dress with a lilac lining. Her long, fair hair shone, so pale it was like moonbeams. Her feet were dainty. She was wearing tiny white ballet shoes with the ribbons laced around her ankles.

'Papa! Papa! Is this Zoë?' She clapped her hands. 'Hello. Zoë. I'm so pleased you've come, let me show you round our island.'

She held out her hand towards Zoë. Zoë looked at Phineas with a puzzled expression.

'I told Roseena I would bring you to meet her. Roseena, don't try to do everything today. Zoë can come again'

'Is it alright for Zoë to meet Mr. Tumblederry and Popcorn?'

Phineas laughed. 'That would certainly be an experience for her. Don't forget, Zoë, that this is another world, so be prepared for some surprises!'

Roseena led Zoë to the path between the trees. The road forked and they took the track to the left. It led to a pretty thatched cottage, surrounded by several small coloured huts: pink, yellow, pale blue.

Roseena led the way, calling out as she reached the open gate. Zoë didn't know whether to laugh or not, as coming out of the cottage was a man. He approached them walking on his hands, wearing gloves made of moccasin, similar to Zoë's Mum's gardening gloves. He was dressed all in green. Even when he reached them, he didn't turn around. His hair was bright orange and looked like the end of a pineapple.

'Mr Tumblederry, this is Zoë my new friend.'

Zoë was thrilled by Roseena's introduction.

'Pleased to meet you, Miss Zoë.' He bent

his right leg down and stretched his bare foot towards Zoë.

Not knowing what to do, Zoë glanced at Roseena, who nodded slightly. So Zoë shook her hand with Mr Tumblederry's foot. He grinned.

'I guess you're not from round here then. Not met a turnabout like me before.'

'Er, no…I'm pleased to meet you too, Mr Tumblederry. I love your cottage.'

'Thank you, have you been here long?'

'No, we came just a few minutes ago. Phineas did bring me once before but only to his house. Roseena brought me to meet you first.'

'Well, that is an honour. I hope you make lots of friends here. I'm sure you will. Phineas doesn't often bring people through his gateway, so he must trust you.'

'Are there other ways to get here then?' Zoë was curious because Mr Tumblederry had referred to Phineas bringing her through "his" gateway, implied there were others.

Mr Tumblederry paused a while, then answered her question. 'Well, yes… but to other dimensions not just yours.'

The more Zoë heard about this fascinating place, the more her head spun.

Roseena touched her arm to bring her back from her daydreaming.

'Zoë, I'd really like you to meet Popcorn today. Is he about, Mr Tumblederry?'

'He should be. Most of your friends will be at The Colourings, but I don't think he's gone yet. Try his hut, the door is open.'

Zoë followed Roseena over the yard towards the huts. Roseena called out as they approached. 'Popcorn are you there?'

Chapter 7
First Impressions

'We must try not to get Popcorn excited, because he… Oh, you'll find out.'

Roseena approached one of the small huts. It had a swinging ranch-style door. As they came closer it opened and Popcorn appeared.

Zoë hadn't expected the small cute dragon. He was yellow, with a lovely tail sweeping behind him. Roseena brought him forward to meet the visitor.

'Zoë, this is Popcorn, he's a dinky dragon, isn't he?'

It was as Zoë and Roseena patted his head, that Popcorn changed colour. First from yellow to orange, then from orange to red. Then, with the excitement of the attention from the girls, a cloud of yellow burst from beneath his tail, which smelt like rotten eggs. Zoë and Roseena backed away pinching their noses. Popcorn's eyes filled with tears and he hung his head. One large tear fell steaming as it splashed on the ground.

Zoë felt so sorry for him. She stepped forward and wiped away his tears with her handkerchief and stroked his wide nose. He lifted his head and looked her in the eye. From that moment on they were firm friends. Popcorn returned to his yellow colour and trotted after the girls as they made their way back to Phineas.

Roseena told Zoë that her friends were all different, some animals, some children, some from other dimensions. Various gateways allowed them to visit Serendipity.

'There are doors, like the grandfather clock you came through, from different worlds. Most creatures return but some chose to stay on the island.'

'Roseena. Where's your mother?'

Roseena stopped abruptly, turning to Zoë. Her eyes were shining. They were like silvery blue pools.

'She's in a dimension called Illusion. Her name is Serafina. I see her sometimes, in my dreams. Phineas cannot take me to see her because he has no permission to visit Illusion any more. When I am older, I will be allowed through the gateway to Illusion to meet her.'

Zoë touched Roseena's shoulder. 'I hope I haven't upset you, Roseena. When will you be able to go?'

'I have to be seven thousand days old, like when you become eighteen or twenty-one earth years.'

Roseena touched the top of her head and swung her long silver hair over her shoulder: 'I must have inherited this from my mother. I always remember her long flowing hair when I wake up, even if I don't remember her face.'

They walked back to the fork in the road, Popcorn following them. The girls left him at the waterfall as they went through to join Phineas.

He was sitting in an arbour in the garden. Zoë sat down next to him. Roseena sat at his feet.

'Well, first impressions of the island are fascinating, aren't they Zoë?'

'I have so many questions, Phineas.' Zoë twisted her handkerchief.

'I'm sure you have. I'll try to answer some now, but your curiosity will never be entirely satisfied. What do you want to know?'

'What are The Colourings?'

Phineas looked down at his daughter.

'Mr Tumblederry mentioned them, not me.'

Phineas turned towards Zoë. 'You've heard people talk about the pot of gold at the end of the rainbow.'

Zoë nodded, waiting for Phineas to continue, her eyes wide.

'No one knows about the other end of the rainbow. "The Colourings" are where all the colours come from. The opposite end of the rainbow holds the colours for everything. Everywhere in nature is mixed from the colours of the rainbow.'

'Wow!' Zoë tried to take in exactly what Phineas was saying.

'I think we should get back now, Zoë.

They said their goodbyes to Roseena. Zoë hugged her and Phineas kissed her forehead.

Soon they were at the lake and rowing across in a small walnut-shaped boat.

They went back through to the shop. Zoë glanced over her shoulder as she walked down the stairs. The grandfather clock still said ten to twelve.

Phineas gave Zoë a small brown envelope with her wages in it and shooed her off home. Waving from the shop door, she called

'Bye, Phineas, and thank you.'

As she turned from the shop door, she sensed someone watching her, she felt uncomfortable.

'There's something wrong here.' She muttered under her breath.

Chapter 8

Zoë is Troubled

Zoë started to walk home. She felt uncomfortable, but didn't know why. She noticed an old lady across the road who looked familiar. Zoë glanced at her again, then remembered where she'd seen her before. It was the lady she'd made her first sale to. The one who had brought the little mantel clock. As soon as the woman realised Zoë had spotted her, she started rummaging in her bag. For some unknown reason, Zoë felt suspicious.

The street wasn't busy but Zoë had to wait for a council dustcart to pass before she could cross the road. She dug her hands into her pockets and approached the woman.

'Hello. Did your sister like her birthday present?' Zoë asked.

'Birthday present? What are you talking about?' she snapped, trying to walk away. Her dark clothes and her abrupt manner seemed menacing.

Zoë followed her. 'The little clock, did your sister like it?'

'Oh, yes, the mantel clock. Got to go, just checking it's still there.'

'What's still there? You brought the mantel clock.'

'No. The antique shop is still here.'

'Of course. Why shouldn't it be?'

'Hasn't moved on yet, there's still time.'

'I don't understand. You sound like you expect Phineas to close down the shop.'

'I must go.' She was walking so briskly, Zoë almost had to run to keep up. 'What did you mean?'

'That would be telling.' The old lady touched the side of her nose. Then she turned the corner into the next street and disappeared. Zoë was left looking around, wondering where she'd gone.

Slowly turning left, Zoë pondered on the conversation she'd just had, trying to analyse it. What did the old woman mean? Something was wrong.

On her way home she relived her time on Serendipity Island, amazed that there was no concept of time there. It was as if you could do anything at whatever pace you wanted to, without having to look at a watch or a clock. No appointments to be on time for. Nobody saying: "Hurry up, you'll be late." Sheer bliss.

Her days at school and home in her true dimension seemed slow and boring. Zoë knew her reality must be faced daily. She found herself starting to take her studies more seriously. She had her visits to Serendipity to look forward to. She wanted to be able to tell Phineas that her new outlook was all because he'd let her visit his island. She couldn't tell him yet though, because she was afraid he'd stop her going there. Also she had to tell Phineas about the suspicious old lady.

★

Her next shift at "Another Dimension" was after school on Thursday.

'I'm off to the shop now Mum.'

'How's it going, Zo?'

'Great, I've made my first sale, a little clock.'

'Well done. That must have felt good.'

'Yeah. It's mostly just cleaning and labelling though. There are some lovely bits and pieces. I might find something for Dad's birthday?'

'That's a good idea. You'd best be going, hadn't you?'

A strong bond had developed between Zoë and Phineas, making her determined to keep the secrets of Serendipity to herself. She'd have to tell her mother more about the shop. It was difficult to hide her excitement about the island.

Phineas was on the telephone when she arrived. He passed her a book about antiques. She moved to the window where there was more light. Instinctively, she glanced across the road and spotted the old woman just as she disappeared into a doorway.

When Phineas had finished his call, Zoë crossed the room and joined him in the back of the shop. 'Do you remember the lady who brought that little mantel clock last week, Phineas?'

'Yes. Why?'

'She keeps watching the shop. When I left you on Saturday, I spoke to her and she acted very weird. She implied you were closing down.' Zoë filled the kettle to make tea. 'I don't really understand it. She's there again today.'

'We'll have to be very careful, Zoë. It can only mean one thing. She knows about Serendipity. Maybe she thinks you don't know.

Whatever happens, don't tell her anything.'

Phineas took a mug from Zoë and continued: 'I think she might be a spy. They must have recruited an agent here.'

'Who are "they" Phineas? Why do they need a spy?'

Phineas sat down behind a big antique desk. Zoë pulled herself up to sit on top of the desk.

' "They" are those who want to claim the secrets of the island. They can't get inside, so may be trying to use outsiders to get access for them.'

'I still don't know who "they" are?'

'The mermaids and mermen.'

'You mean they really exist, mermaids and mermen.' Zoë jumped down from the desk.

'I shouldn't be surprised, really, after my visit to your island. Are they a threat, then?'

'Yes. They've found their way as far as Lake Tanamere, but they can't get into the island. They try to entice the children away.'

'Are they dangerous? I know the legend about them singing to call sailors to their death at sea.'

'No, not dangerous, but they are cunning. The problem is they sing beautiful songs which can be quite mesmerising. They tempt the children with charms and gifts. The mermaids swim across many oceans, bringing treasures from far-off lands.'

'Phineas, what will the spy do?'

'I think she'll try to follow you. Be very careful, Zoë.'

'I will. I think I'd better do some work, hadn't I?'

Phineas smiled. He gave her a pen and notepad and pointed to a pile of old books. 'Can you list the titles and authors, please?'

Zoë took the pen and pad and picking up the first book, started her task.

'And Zoë, next time you come, I'll take you to "The Colourings." Then you'll understand why the secrets of Serendipity have to be protected.'

Chapter 9

The Carnival

At five o'clock Zoë was still sitting on the floor sorting the books. Phineas tapped her on the shoulder and told her it was time to go home. She stood up, tying her sweater around her waist and grabbing her school bag from under the desk. She said "'Bye" to Phineas and started towards the shop door.

Phineas picked up the list Zoe had made from the desk and called after her. 'See you Saturday morning and we'll go to Serendipity.'

Zoë punched the air with her fist. 'I can't wait to see Roseena, Popcorn and Mr Tumblederry.'

'You'll be able to see a lot more this time, Zoë. I promise you will have a really exciting time at "The Colourings."'

Zoë left "Another Dimension" a few minutes later, glancing left, right and across the road, searching for "the spy." She heaved a sigh of relief, satisfied there was no sign of the woman she now considered a threat.

★

On Saturday they wasted no time in making their way through the grandfather clock. It was only five minutes after nine when Zoë closed the door panel behind them. She looked across the lake at the beautiful island. Phineas was already in the nutshell boat, holding the oars. Zoë stepped in and in no time they were gliding across the shimmering lake.

'Are there any mermaids around?' Zoë whispered, her eyes searching the waters around them.

'Don't worry. They can't get to this side of the island. There's a dam about half a mile one way and an extremely high waterfall the other.'

They stepped out of the boat and Phineas led the way. As they passed through the garden behind Phineas' house, Roseena met them, carrying a picnic basket. She was obviously excited. She ran to Zoë, passing the basket to her father. Grabbing Zoë's hand, she dragged her towards the waterfall. As they went through, she called over her shoulder to

Phineas: 'See you over there.'

She continued to run towards Mr Tumblederry's cottage. Zoë tripped, steadied herself and followed. When they arrived at the cottage, Mr Tumblederry was waiting at the gate. Zoë stopped to greet him, as Roseena ran past him.

'Popcorn has already gone, Zoë. You'll see him there. I think Roseena is rather impatient. I'll see you later.' He cartwheeled back to his cottage door, waving his toes as he went.

Zoë followed Roseena around the back of the huts where Popcorn lived. The next surprise was a corral of beautiful animals. There were snow-white unicorns, silver winged horses, graceful gazelles, coloured striped zebras and colour patched giraffes. Roseena blew a tiny whistle and a winged horse approached them.

'The Colourings are at the centre of the island. My pony, Mercury, will take us.'

The pale silver pony knelt down and both girls climbed onto his broad back. Zoë held her breath as the winged horse flew upwards. It was exhilarating. At first Zoë had her eyes squeezed tight. When she opened them and saw the huge wingspan of the horse, she relaxed to enjoy the experience.

Looking down she saw the lush beauty of

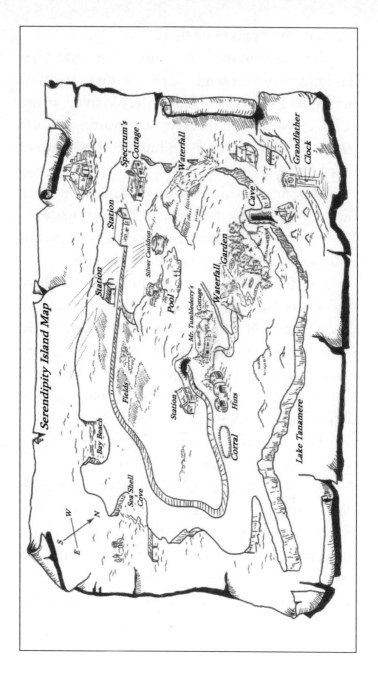

Serendipity Island Map

the island. 'This is so cool, Roseena. It must be heaven to live here.'

Soon they were descending into a clearing which was a hive of activity, excitement and colour. It was like a carnival. Beautiful music filled the air. Aromas tantalized the nostrils, making them hungry. Mercury landed and the girls slipped down next to a stall covered with a bright blue canopy. Underneath sat Phineas. He offered them glasses of a sweet nectar drink.

'How did you get here, Phineas?' asked Zoë, curious that, as they'd flown here, how come Phineas was here quicker?

'Ah, Zoë. The mysteries of our island confuse you. Another unexpected twist, why am I here first? I came another way, via the mole tunnel mines.'

Roseena put down her empty glass on a tray, taking Zoë's from her, she insisted they go.

The carnival atmosphere was electric. It was like a fun fair and a circus. There were masses of people and animals everywhere. Jugglers, clowns and a young girl with a group of coloured poodles: pink, lilac and blue. Two men walked past on green and white striped stilts. Gymnasts practiced their somersaults, wearing orange leotards. Roseena pointed to the horse riders on coloured horses: red, yellow, purple and pink.

The kiosks were offering sweet smelling snacks, new to Zoë. She tried a cake that looked like a meringue. As it dissolved on her tongue it tasted of raspberry and caramel. Zoë was excited. The colours were the most overwhelming part for her. Roseena led her to a fountain.

'Look at the birds, Zoë.'

There were so many different species of birds dipping their feathers in the water, the colours glistened. They walked like models on a catwalk. Peacocks with their fantails, colourful parrots and macaws, tiny humming birds and lovebirds, even a phoenix with fiery feathers sparking like fireworks.

Zoë whispered to Roseena: 'I wish I had my camcorder to capture this. It's fantastic.'

They waved to Mr Tumblederry, who was having his toenails painted a fluorescent green by an elegant ostrich. She held the fine brush in her beak.

To their left was a pool where a team of large turquoise seahorses and a team of red flying fish were playing water polo.

To the right of the fountain was an enormous silver cauldron, with tiny taps around the base. Roseena pointed to the cauldron. 'My father will tell you all about that later. It's where the colours come from. Can you see at the top? There's the rainbow.'

Zoë looked up. She saw where the rainbow dipped into the huge shiny pot.

'Wow. I can't believe I'm seeing this.'

Roseena tapped Zoë's arm. 'Look.'

Trotting towards them came Popcorn, colours changing from yellow…orange…red. Puff! Yellow smoke billowed. The girls held their noses, giggled and hugged Popcorn before he got upset.

Phineas joined them.

'Come on Zoë. You should meet the Spectrum family. They're responsible for the rainbow colours. I think you'll be fascinated.'

Chapter 10
The Spectrum Family

The colours around them were vivid. Zoe's home seemed like those black and white sepia photographs she'd seen in Phineas' shop. This was in Technicolor. Zoë and Roseena almost had to run to keep up with Phineas as he walked briskly towards the Spectrum's house.

Zoë saw the cottage up ahead, up being the appropriate word as it stood on a small hill. It reminded her of the fairytale books of her early childhood. The family were in the garden having a picnic.

Phineas called out: 'Opal, can we join you?'

A stocky, motherly woman turned towards them. She beamed at Phineas, beckoning with her hands enthusiastically for them to come in. 'You've brought your visitor, I see. Hello there. Welcome to the mad house.'

'Hi, kids. This is Zoë,' shouted Phineas, waving.

The children smiled, waved or mumbled greetings. Opal Spectrum led them to the table she had set up in front of the cottage, handing them all a plate. She gestured for them to help themselves. The table was laden with cooked meats, fish, cheese, pasties, quiches, pies and delicious looking desserts.

'Opal is an excellent cook, Zoë. Here, try this steak and mushroom pie. I don't know what her secret recipe is but it's my favourite.'

Phineas cut a slice and placed it on Zoë's plate. Then he added a spoonful of rice with green peas, sweetcorn and cashew nuts.

Roseena offered Zoë a chicken drumstick covered in a sweet satay sauce. 'This is delicious.' she said, choosing another chicken drumstick for herself.

Zoë added some crusty bread and cheese.

'Let's sit down and eat, shall we?' suggested Phineas. 'I'd recommend the strawberry and chocolate dessert after.' He nudged Zoë's arm. He pressed his fingertips to his lips, in a gesture expressing pure delight.

Opal led them to some chairs under a multi-coloured parasol. 'My husband, Laser, will be back shortly, he's just fetching some buckets before anyone starts collecting their colours this afternoon.'

Zoë looked puzzled and Phineas quickly explained.

'You'll see later. Everyone brings containers to collect the colour they need from the cauldron.

'Zoë, this is my eldest daughter, Ruby,' said Opal.

Ruby brought them a tray of drinks in coloured plastic cups. She wore a red sleeveless dress and a red bandana.

It suddenly occurred to Zoë, as she glanced round at the rest of the family, that they were all dressed in different colours. She wasn't surprised, when she asked their names, they reflected their respective colours.

Opal pointed to a girl sitting cross-legged, with her plate in her lap. 'That's Amber.'

She wore an orange apron over a paler orange dress. Ruby and Amber had red hair. Ruby's was a rich auburn, while Amber's was a more subtle strawberry blonde.

'What about the two boys playing "tig" around the flagpole.' Zoë nodded towards the boys chasing each other, as she sampled the chicken.

One wore yellow and one green: T-shirts, shorts and baseball caps. At the top of the flagpole a rainbow banner fluttered in the breeze.

'My twin boys: Topaz and Emerald, they're nick named Topi and Emmy.' Opal handed Zoë a serviette to wipe her sticky fingers.

'And the little sweetheart on the swing?'

'Sapphire, come and say hello to Zoë.'

She was swinging on a colourful hammock. A delicate looking child with shoulder length ash-blonde hair. She pirouetted across the garden to show off her blue swirling skirt and top.

'She's our little dancer,' Opal explained.

'Where's Indi?' asked Roseena.

'He's with Laser. Ah! Here they come now.'

As father and son approached, Roseena ran off to meet them. Indi was a tall, dark, good-looking teenager. He wore a dark blue sweater and jeans.

Zoë felt her jacket sleeve being pulled from behind her chair. She turned around to see a head peeping out. It was a little girl of about five years old, wearing purple dungarees and a lilac straw sunhat covering her golden curls.

'I'm Amy.'

Her mother saw Zoë bending down. She got up and, holding Amy's hand, brought her round to see Zoë.

'Her full name is Amethyst. It's a bit of a

mouthful for her. She's the youngest.' Opal lifted Amy on to her lap, as Laser, Indi and Roseena joined them.

'Laser, this is Zoë.' Phineas stood up and shook hands with the tall, handsome man. He reminded Zoë of a film star but she couldn't remember which one.

'What a colourful family!' Zoë couldn't help remarking to Roseena, as she nibbled at the food from her plate. Roseena and Zoë giggled as they saw Popcorn plodding up the hill. When he arrived he plonked himself in front of the group, pawing the ground. It was Phineas that spotted the note tucked into his collar.

Chapter 11

The Silver Cauldron

The note was a message scrawled in spidery writing. It was from Mr Tumblederry, informing Laser there was a queue forming at the cauldron. Not that he needed to hurry, just a gentle reminder. Indi and Laser filled plates with food to take with them. As they decided to go. The Spectrum family led the way.

'Hang on a minute Zoë. I'll explain on the way what this is all about,' said Phineas.

Roseena excused herself to walk with Indi. Opal closed the cottage door and reassured everyone that Popcorn was on guard duty. This made Popcorn puff out a small flame, showing his authority.

Phineas told Zoë: 'Only the Spectrum family are allowed to touch the cauldron. It is their responsibility to keep it topped up. The children have to collect water from the waterfall and keep the levels above the floats which indicate how high the water is. They also have to keep the cauldron shiny outside and check the taps work properly. Only Laser and Opal can dispense colours.'

When they arrived at the cauldron, Zoë saw the queue. All sorts of people and animals were waiting with an assortment of vessels. Some as small as test tubes, to saucepans and kettles, to buckets and watering cans. They were all chattering and singing. A bandstand had an orchestra of strange creatures playing various instruments. An octopus played three instruments: a trumpet, an accordion and a set of bongo drums. Two monkeys played together on a piano. The atmosphere was exhilarating.

Zoë and Phineas watched from the side of the cauldron.

'Can you see those little corks bobbing in that pipe, Zoë?' Phineas took Zoë close to the cauldron, pointing to one of the clear pipes that surrounded the pot.

'There are seven pipes, one for each colour of the spectrum. The water has to be above the line indicated by a coloured mark.

'Why do they need the colours, Phineas?'

'Not all worlds are like yours, Zoë. You have sun and rain, which make things grow. In some worlds the colours have to be painted in, like a picture. Then, sometimes, the people and animals just want to change the normal colour, to be different, and here it's possible.'

Laser banged on a huge brass gong. Then Opal and Laser started opening the taps at the base of the cauldron to fill the vessels.

Zoë heard each one call out which colour they wanted as they approached the front of the queue.

'Red, Orange, Yellow, Green, Blue, Indigo, Violet,' all the colours of the rainbow above. The end of the arc dipped into the top of the huge silver cauldron.

A small grey squirrel called out 'Red, I want to be a red squirrel.'

A rabbit hopped forward carrying a basket of white flowers and a small can. 'Yellow, I have to paint the primroses yellow.'

A clown in a harlequin outfit with a huge bucket, shouted 'Violet. I've run out of violet for my collapsible car.'

'Wow…this is something else!' Zoë exclaimed, as she watched the colours flow from the taps. It occurred to her that although it was only water being put in at the top, yet colours came out of the base. 'Magical! No wonder this had to be protected.'

Zoë leaned closer to Phineas and whispered: 'Phineas…is this what the mermaids want?'

'Well, they don't know this is here. We think they are after the pot of gold.'

Phineas drew Zoë away from the others. 'Legend has it that the pot of gold never runs dry. As that is the only story that has leaked out, we're almost sure that's what they're after.'

'Why doesn't someone tell them it's not here?' asked Zoë, puzzled that it was such an easy solution.

'They have never actually communicated with anyone. They just try to invade us. We have such strong defences though. They'll never get into the island.'

Phineas and Zoë walked around behind the queue. They sat by the bandstand, watching as the colours flowed from the cauldron, and Phineas continued explaining: 'There are birds in the air who alert the pterodactyl to attack if necessary. The water has its own defence team ready to send the sharks, who are normally harmless, but when it comes to mermaids and mermen, they hate them.'

'Where's Roseena?' asked Indi and Ruby, as they joined them on the steps of the bandstand.

'I thought she was with you, Indi.' replied Phineas.

'Oh, she'll probably turn up in a minute. Zoë, I think I'd better get you back. We'll go via the mole tunnels.'

Zoë stood up and waved to her new friends. She put out her hand to pull Phineas up.

'Thanks, Zoë. See you folks later. Tell Roseena to stay with you till I get back, will you?'

'Right-O, Uncle Phineas,' said Indi.

Zoë followed as Phineas led the way to the small railway station, where little carriages waited to transport them underground. The carriages looked like peapods. There was room for just two people in each pod.

'Are you really their uncle?'

'Yes. Laser is my brother.'

The pod started up and moved downwards into caves. After a few hundred yards, Zoë started to notice changes in the structure of the walls. It glistened and sparkled. Phineas pointed out first the quartz crystals then, as they went deeper, he showed her amethyst, blue topaz and pink sapphire, even some diamonds.

'Unfortunately, we can't take things through to your world Zoë. So you won't be

able to get your mother a present here.'

Little glowworms and fireflies lit the caves like tiny stars. There never seemed to be an end to the secrets this island concealed.

Phineas and Zoë stepped out of their carriage at a small hut near Mr Tumblederry's cottage. As soon as they emerged out of the station, an odd-looking bird flew down from a tree. It looked like a large pigeon but was blue with a silver collar. Zoë wasn't really surprised when it started to speak.

'Phineas, trouble's brewing. They've got Roseena.'

Chapter 12

Roseena is Missing

'Oh, no! I knew something like this would happen! What do they say?'

Phineas was obviously upset. Zoë didn't know what to do.

'Nothing. No demands, no threats, just a message in a bottle, thrown into the lake.'

The bird flew up to retrieve a satchel from the tree. He hooked his head through the strap and brought it back to Phineas, who tipped out the small green bottle with a piece of parchment in it. Phineas took the message and read it. Just as the bird said, only the words: 'We've got the girl,' were printed in squid ink.

'Look Zoë I have get you back quickly. I need to find Roseena.'

'I'll stay and help, Phineas.'

'No Zoë.'

He led her back, through the waterfall into his garden.

'Maybe later. When we know more. They won't hurt her, that wouldn't get them anywhere, would it?'

'No, but I want to help. Please, Phineas, let me know what's happening?'

Phineas took Zoë back across the lake. If he hadn't insisted on taking her, she would have tried to stay. Back through the clock, Zoë was still trying to persuade him to let her do something.

'Look, my dear. You know we're in different time zones. As soon as I know anything, I'll get a message to you somehow.'

He rushed off, back towards the lake.

Zoë ran down the stairs, out of the shop, slamming the door as she left.

She crossed the road in a daze, not really concentrating. Automatically she'd checked for traffic. So she didn't see the woman until she was right in front of her.

'So, you know they've got the girl?' the woman hissed in Zoë's face.

Zoë pondered on her first impressions of this little old woman. She wasn't the nice refined lady she'd appeared to be. Another case of appearances can be deceptive.

Zoë stepped back. 'You witch! Where is she? What do they want?'

'Oh. She's safe. She'll be fine, as long as they get the pot of gold.' The woman wagged her finger at Zoë. 'And you're the one to get it for them.'

'What are you on about?' Zoë was starting to panic. She didn't want to be dragged into this.

The woman grabbed Zoë's arm. 'If they want the girl back, you've got to take the pot of gold to Sea Shell Cove, where the mermen will meet you.

Zoë wanted to help Roseena, but didn't know how. She was scared. 'Let me go,' she screamed. 'I can't help.'

'Well, you'll have to find someone who can, won't you?' cackled the old woman, letting go of Zoë's arm and backing away with a menacing look on her face, which made Zoë tremble with fear.

'If you don't get them the pot of gold, they're going to take the girl to Merlandia. She'll become a mermaid. She'd never return.'

Zoë turned and ran in the direction of home. She didn't stop until she got back to her house. Unlocking the front door, she ran upstairs to her room. Flinging herself onto her bed, she wondered how on earth she was going to help Roseena. She'd have to go back and tell Phineas. The problem was how? The shop was closed and Phineas was on Serendipity Island. Zoë didn't know how to contact him. She wondered what was happening over there?

'Zoë, lunch is ready.' Her mum called up the stairs.

'O.K. I'm coming.' Zoë ran down stairs and into the kitchen.

Zoë's Dad was still at work, so there were just the two of them.

'You alright, Zo?'

'Yeah… actually no. I'm worried about Phineas.'

She had to be very careful what she said to her parents, who still knew nothing about Serendipity.

'Well, ring him after lunch then'

'He won't be at the shop though.' Zoë mumbled. 'Anyway I don't know the number.'

'It will be in the phone book. You can leave a message,' suggested her mum.

'I suppose so.' It was worth a try.

After their meal Zoë went to look for a phone book. She was expecting it to be an unlisted number, but there in the Yellow Pages under Antique shops, she found it: "Another Dimension."

She checked her mum was still in the kitchen, washing up, closed the kitchen door and dialled the number. After three rings the answer phone clicked in. Phineas' voice stated 'Another Dimension' is closed, please leave a message after the beep' Zoë hesitated, then realised she had to try anything.

'Phineas this is Zoë, please can you call me, my mobile number is… it's about our problem.'

Zoë didn't really think this was going to be any use, but what else could she do?'

She decided she'd have to act. Maybe it would be worth surfing the Internet. She booted up the computer, connected to the Internet and typed in "mermaids." Apart from luring sailors with their singing, she knew very little about them. They'd just been a fairytale.

She spent an hour trying to find something useful. How was she going to help get Roseena back? No pot of gold, but how could she prove there wasn't, without telling them there was something even more exciting?

Her research only told of the vanity of mermaids.

Her mobile started ringing. Zoë picked it up and answered.

'Hello. Zoë. It's Phineas. I got your message. What's wrong?'

'Oh. Phineas. Any news your end first?'

'No. Nothing. No demands. Nothing.'

'Oh… that means I'm the go-between.'

'What do you mean, Zoë?'

'That old woman, she grabbed me when I left you. Look I've got to see you. Can you meet me?'

'Oh Zoë, I'm so sorry they've got you involved. I'll be at the shop when you get here. I just want to get Roseena back.'

Zoë could tell by his voice that he was upset. She just hoped her plan would work.

By now it was late afternoon. She crept into her father's study, found the family's video camera and put it in her sports bag. Jumping down the stairs, she grabbed her coat from the hall, calling to her Mum.

'I'll be about an hour, Mum. I'm going to see Phineas.'

Knowing her time on Serendipity would stand still here, she only needed time to get to the shop and back. She banged the front door shut and raced off down the street.

Chapter 13

Mermaids and Mermen

Zoë arrived at "Another Dimension," within fifteen minutes of her conversation with Phineas.

The shop door was open. She stepped inside, putting the catch down on the door as she closed it. She took the golden mirror and comb out of the window, and put them in her bag. Phineas was waiting for her, looking worried. Zoë couldn't help herself; she rushed up to him and flung her arms around him.

'It's O.K. They won't hurt her. You were right they want the pot of gold, but we're really going to have to prove it's not here.'

Zoë led the way up the stairs to the clock. She continued telling Phineas about the confrontation with "that wicked woman" and also about the Merfolks threat. They stepped into a small nutshell boat.

'I think I've got a plan but I'm not sure if it will work.'

Zoë helped Phineas row across Lake Tanamere.

Phineas listened as Zoë told him of her Internet research about mermaids.

'Do you remember that lovely mirror and comb that you have in the shop? Well. I brought them with me; we could use them to tempt the mermaids at the cove. Then we can tell them the pot of gold isn't here.'

They arrived at Serendipity quicker with both of them rowing. Phineas used the prism key to dissolve the bubble wall. Once they were through, the barrier was restored. The sunlight glistened on its surface.

'I don't think that our word will be enough, Zoë. The mermen are not going to believe us.'

'Then we go to plan B.'

Zoë related her plan as they walked towards Phineas' house and through the garden.

'Do you think that would be proof enough, Phineas?'

'It just might work. Zoë. It's worth a try.'

'We will try the mermaids first though, maybe we can save ourselves a lot of work if they believe us.'

'Do you want to go to Seashell Cove first?'

71

'Yeah. How do we get there?'

They walked as far as Mr Tumblederry's cottage. Just as they reached his gate, he came out walking on his hands.

'Any news?' Phineas asked hopefully.

'Nope. We haven't told the kids. They think she's with Zoë.'

Zoë pulled at Phineas' sleeve.

'Let's go, this isn't getting Roseena back.'

Phineas took a large handkerchief from his pocket and wiped his eyes. Then waved it like a white flag of surrender.

They climbed into a green peapod carriage, taking the railway to Sea Shell Cove. It was in the opposite direction to the journey Zoë had taken the last time.

They travelled quickly along the cliff paths for about a mile. They hardly noticed the beautiful scenery as they discussed the plan.

'It was my research on the Internet that gave me the idea.'

'That's something you won't find on Serendipity – computers.'

'Yes, I know, but Phineas, there's much more to offer here than technology.'

They travelled downwards emerging in a cave. Zoë stepped out of the carriage on to soft white sand. The cove was breathtaking, reminding her of a travel advertisement for an exotic holiday. Her mother would love this.

Zoë explained what she wanted to do, as she looked round the beach for a suitable place.

'We need somewhere jutting out into the sea.'

'What about over here, Zoë?' Phineas led Zoë around a large boulder, where there was a short pier.

Zoë took the golden comb and mirror out of her bag. She sat cross-legged on the edge of the jetty, combing her hair and holding the mirror up high.

'Phineas, have you got your flute with you?' she called over her shoulder.

'Yes. Why?' He took it from his coat pocket.

'We'll need to attract their attention.' She whispered pointing out to sea. 'Then I'll leave the comb and mirror to tempt the mermaids.'

Phineas whistled first an Irish jig, then a slow waltz on his flute. Zoë continued combing her hair as she watched across the water. Their patience was eventually rewarded. Zoë left the comb and mirror on the edge of the wooden pier. She gestured with her hand to Phineas to move behind the boulder. They were able to watch discretely what would happen.

As the waters rippled, a head appeared a few yards away. It was a mermaid. Zoë had expected a beautiful golden-haired female. She was very pale, her skin was almost translucent and her hair, which had floated on the surface of the water, clung to her body as she reached up to take the comb.

Zoë and Phineas crept round, watching the mermaid as she picked up the mirror. Then she started combing her hair.

Zoë called softly to her: 'Hi, I'm Zoë.'

The mermaid turned.

'Please could you give a message to your people? They have my friend, Roseena.'

The mermaid looked all around for who was speaking. Zoë held her hand up to Phineas to stop him going further. She approached the pier then stopped.

'How can we get Roseena back?'

The mermaid shrugged her shoulders and shook her head. Still holding the comb and mirror she swam away.

Zoë saw her silvery-green tail flip, the scales shining as they caught the sunlight.

'The message is: " there is no pot of gold at this end of the rainbow, it's not here." Please ask them to bring Roseena back.' Zoë shouted after her.

The mermaid stopped, made some strange gestures with her hands. She pointed out to sea, and then disappeared beneath the surface of the water.

Zoë walked back to Phineas. 'We'll just have to wait a while, see whether she tells them.'

Zoë rolled up her jeans and took off her trainers, stuffing her socks inside them. She paddled along the edge of the shoreline.

Phineas watched Zoë then looked out to sea. 'Zoë, look. I think there's something happening.'

Zoë squinted in the sunlight. She could see several heads bobbing through the water. As they came nearer, Zoë and Phineas walked to the end of the pier.

One merman approached them. In a gravelly voice he called out, 'We know the legend is true; there's a pot of gold at the end of the rainbow. This is it. If you want the girl, that's the deal.'

He threw the golden comb and mirror onto the beach. Zoë was so frustrated she picked up a pebble and considered throwing it at the merman. Phineas grabbed her hand and frowned. She dropped the pebble at her feet.

Phineas took a step forward.

'It's my daughter you have. Please don't hurt her. I assure you she is worth more to me than gold. It really isn't here.'

'Prove it.' The merman challenged them. 'Or we keep the girl.'

'Looks like we have to use our alterative plan then, Phineas.'

Chapter 14

There's No Pot of Gold

Zoë took more notice of the scenery this time, as they travelled across the island by rail. She tried to distract Phineas by asking him questions about the island.

'Are those sunflowers painted blue from the silver cauldron?'

'No. They're not like your sunflowers. Ours are a different colour every day. Seven days of the week, seven colours of the rainbow.'

They travelled through fields of corn with red, blue and purple poppies. Green fields with sheep, their wool already coloured. Then Zoë spotted a cow. 'Is that a cow naturally bright crimson or painted?'

'Betty is special. She really is red today, isn't she? When we feed her strawberries she gives us strawberry flavoured milk.'

Zoë licked her lips.

'Mm…So if you gave her chocolate, would she give hot chocolate?'

'Er… The kids tried feeding her cocoa beans once. She didn't like them and the field was rather well fertilized that day, if you know what I mean. The cowpats were huge. Poor Betty.'

Zoë laughed. She would have liked to video the island, but she knew Phineas would not allow her to. She didn't want to upset him. He must be worrying about Roseena.

When they arrived at the Spectrum's, Laser and Opal were waiting.

'What's happening, Phineas?' Laser helped Zoë out of the peapod carriage, taking her sports bag from her.

'We have to prove there's no pot of gold. Zoë's got an idea. I just hope it works.'

Opal beckoned them into the cottage. The four of them sat around the kitchen table, drinking a sweet, minty juice.

'Oh, my poor Roseena. What can be happening to her? Where are they keeping her?'

Opal put her hand on Phineas' hand.

'She'll be fine. The merfolk won't harm her if they want to trade her, now will they?'

'But they're threatening to take her to Merlandia.'

Laser looked across at Zoë, quickly changing the subject. 'What's your plan then young lady?'

Zoë briefly outlined her idea.

Opal gathered up the glasses: 'Let's get moving then. The sooner we do this the better. I'll get the children, but I'm not telling them why.'

Laser nodded.

Zoë and Phineas agreed to say nothing about Roseena. They knew it would be difficult.

Zoë picked up her bag, hoping Indi didn't ask where Roseena was. As they made their way down the hill, Opal told her that Laser had sent Indi and Ruby on some errand so they couldn't ask questions.

Laser and Phineas carried a stepladder. Amber and Amy, Emmy and Topi were sent to collect plastic buckets and watering cans of water from the fountain.

Zoë got out the video camera. 'Where do you think I should film from?'

Laser and Phineas set up the step ladder a couple of metres from the cauldron.

'Here should do. Up you go Zoë.' Phineas

steadied the steps, while she climbed.

The children returned with the water. Laser waved them over.

'Right kids; just pour the water in the top while Zoë video's. Wait while she gets ready.'

The children stood on a couple of stools and chairs. Looking up at Zoë, they waited for her signal.

'Be careful, Zoë.' Phineas called. 'Only the top on video – remember.'

'O.K. Kids ready, steady…'

Zoë held the camera, positioned it so she could see the display clearly. She filmed the top of the rainbow as it dipped into the cauldron. Then she raised her hand, dropping it to signal the kids to pour water.

Amy watched the boys.

Emmy and Topi just threw their buckets of water into the pot. Topi threw his yellow bucket on the floor. Emmy got down from his stool with his green bucket.

Amber poured water from an orange jug, smiling towards the camera. Zoë gave her the thumbs up.

Laser held Amy up. She giggled as she sprinkled the water from her purple watering can.

Topi and Emmy had refilled their buckets

and stood on the stools ready to do it again. Then they looked at each other with cheeky grins and threw the buckets of water over each other instead. Zoë captured it all on video. Then she pressed the pause button and climbed down the steps.

'I think this is going to work. Even the boys water-fight.'

She beckoned the others to see. Phineas and Laser stood behind her, while Opal sat on the steps. Zoë rewound the tape and pressed play.

The video of the children playing with water at the end of the rainbow, looked like a children's playground.

'It looks good to me. What do you think Phineas?' Laser patted Zoë's shoulder.

'I just hope the mermen believe what they see and I get my Roseena back.'

'Well, let's go then.' Zoë switched off the camera, put it in her bag and called to the kids:

'Thanks kids. Come on Phineas.'

They left the Spectrum family at the cauldron and walked past the deserted bandstand towards the station.

'I'm going to ask Everett to take us back to the cove, Zoë. Wait here by the station.'

Zoë waited as Phineas walked across the

track to a field. She sat on a bench on the platform. As her back was to the field she didn't see Phineas returning.

'Zoë. We're ready to go. Everett is going to fly us to Sea Shell Cove.'

Zoë stood up and as she turned she stepped back. There behind Phineas was a giant bird. She was speechless and a little scared.

'Are you all right, Zoë. Everett is our friendly transport. He's an eagle-dragon cross.'

Everett had the head of a golden eagle and the body of a dragon. His huge tail was long and thick.

'Shall we go? Have you got the camera?'

Zoë grabbed her bag from under the bench and slung it over her shoulder. Phineas helped Zoë on to the eagon's back and then climbed up behind her.

Soon they were flying across the island, not too high, just above the treetops.

Everett landed on the beach.

'You wait in the cave, Everett. If there's any trouble you can go and get help.'

Phineas and Zoë walked round the boulder towards the jetty. Zoë sat on a rock. Phineas got out his flute. Before he started to play, Zoë heard him mutter.

'I hope this works.'

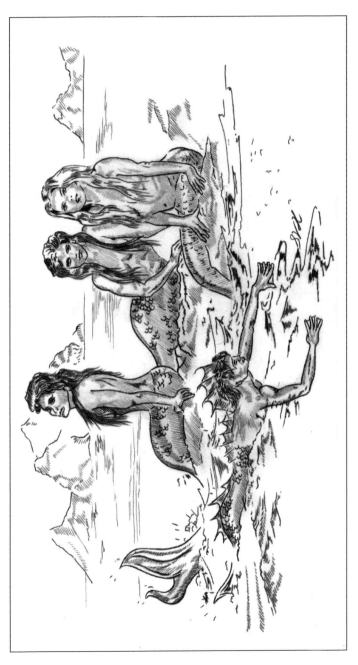

After a few tunes, Phineas stopped, asking: 'Aren't they coming?'

Zoë held her hand over her eyes and peered into the distance. 'Hang on. There's some movement over there.' She pointed to the left. As the merfolk swam nearer, Zoë could see there were three mermaids and two mermen.

The merman they'd met previously came closer. He had matted hair like seaweed and his teeth had bits of fish stuck between them. Zoë didn't like him.

'I can't see any proof Hu man.'

Phineas and Zoë approached the end of the pier. Phineas motioned the merman nearer.

'Where's Roseena, first?'

'She's safe in the next cove.' He pointed to the West. His voice gurgled like water down a plughole.

'Everett – check Roseena is at Bay Beach cove.'

When Everett appeared the merman backed away.

Zoë and Phineas looked at each other. The eagon flew off. When he was out of sight, the merman swam back towards the jetty. Zoë got out the camera.

'No! If you kill me, you'll never get the girl

back.' He suddenly dived down into the sea. The other merfolk disappeared beneath the surface.

Chapter 15

Celebration

'What now?'

Zoë stood up. She was still holding the video camera ready. They waited, wondering what to do next Suddenly, there was a splash. Zoë jumped back as the merman reappeared at the side of the wooden jetty.

'Show me the proof.'

Zoë bent down. Turning the view screen towards him. 'This is a camera. If you look here, you will see pictures of this end of the rainbow.'

She pressed play. The merman peered at the small video image.

'Can you see the children playing?'

Phineas and Zoë watched his face as he stared at the kids having fun with water at the end of the rainbow.

There was a long pause. The silence was

only broken by the rippling of the waves on the sand.

With a blank expression, the merman glanced up at them. He signalled to the others. The Merfolk swam away.

'Looks like we need to travel a long way, to the other end of the rainbow, if we can ever find it?'

He made no apology. He turned and, with a flick of a barnacle covered tail, he disappeared. At the same time Everett appeared with Roseena on his back. Phineas and Zoë went to greet them. Roseena jumped down and ran into her father's arms.

'Zoë, we can never thank you enough.' Phineas's eyes were full of tears.

Roseena had not been harmed and, although upset at being kidnapped, she said she was treated kindly by the mermaids. Everett was sent ahead with the good news to Opal and Laser.

On their way back across the island by rail, Roseena told them how the mermaids had fed and cared for her.

'Roseena, the children don't know what's happened because we didn't want to frighten them.' Phineas sat with his hand on Roseena's shoulder. Zoë was in the next green peapod carriage, putting the camera in her bag. She gave father and daughter time together.

When they arrived back at the Spectrum's, there stood Laser waving a multi-coloured flag. Opal held her arms out to Roseena and gave her a huge hug.

'Let's have a party. Can we, Auntie Opal?'

'Give me a couple of days to prepare, Roseena. I think you should rest now and Zoë needs to go home.'

Laser was talking to Phineas.

'Zoë, Laser and I feel we should destroy your film. You do understand, don't you?'

'Of course.' Zoë fumbled in her bag. She took out the camera and removing the tape, she gave it to Laser.

'Papa. Can Zoë come to the party?'

'Of course. If it wasn't for Zoë, we wouldn't be having the celebration. She'll have to ask at home if she can help me in the shop. If so, she'll be most welcome.'

'I'll make it somehow.' Zoë wasn't going to miss all the fun.

'Opal, shall we say Tuesday, after Zoë finishes school?'

'That sounds fine. Roseena and my girls can help.'

'Come on then Zoë, let's get you back to reality, my girl.'

Phineas took Zoë back all the way around the island, in a small boat pulled by large seahorses. Zoë felt she was on a fairground ride, as they bobbed up and down at speed across the water.

When they arrived back at the harbour, Phineas stayed in the boat. 'You know your way Zoë. I can trust you to go home safely. Make sure the shop door is closed, will you?'

She stepped out of the boat, patting the nearest seahorse.

'Come to the shop after school Tuesday, Zoë. I must get back to Roseena. Gee up.'

Zoë left through the clock as usual and was back home within the hour, but she was very tired.

★

The next few days dragged. On Tuesday Zoë found it very difficult to concentrate. She'd told her mother she was going to the shop straight from school. When she arrived, Phineas was waiting for her.

'Shall we go then? You can leave your school bag here, if you want to.' Phineas pointed to the kitchen.

'Yeah. I'm not lugging this lot with me.'

Zoë shrugged off her coat and threw it over a chair. They were soon on their way. First by boat to the nearest cove, then they took an underground tunnel to the centre of the island. When they got out of the peapod carriage, Zoë could hear music.

'Sounds like the party's starting.' Phineas smiled at Zoë.

'The smaller children don't know about Roseena's ordeal. She told Indi and Ruby. They're very protective of her.'

'Do they know the whole story about the merfolk and proving there's no pot of gold?'

'Yes, Zoë. You're a heroine.'

They'd reached the bandstand by now. There were more musicians playing today. Birds were sitting around the top of the bandstand, singing. Mr Tumblederry was pretending to conduct with a baton between his toes. When he saw Phineas and Zoë he grinned, waving the baton at them.

Opal and some of the circus and fairground folk had prepared enough food for an army. There were games and races in the field next to the fountain. Roseena came running towards them. She hugged Zoë.

'Let's have some fun, Zoë. After, you know what, I just want to forget.'

'Are you really O.K. Roseena?'

Yeah. Fine. What about a ride on the carousel? I know we're a bit old – but who cares?'

The huge roundabout was a circular base with real animals standing on it, giving the children rides to the music playing on the bandstand. Roseena climbed on to a pink elephant, tickling its ears.

A camel knelt down while Zoë scrambled on its back. She felt like a four-year-old at the fairground for the first time. Even the smell of candyfloss and donuts added to the holiday atmosphere.

Everyone was singing and dancing. The girls laughed as Phineas and Laser did an Irish jig, while Indi and Ruby covered their heads with embarrassment. The younger children and their animal friends played cricket. Opal supervised the food and drink, joining in the singing, with two tiny lovebirds sitting on the brim of her large sunhat.

Zoë and Roseena sat on the steps of the bandstand with plates of food and watched Sapphire dancing in her pale blue tutu and ballet shoes.

'She's so sweet. Bless her. I love your family, Roseena.'

Phineas came and sat beside them. 'It's time

to go, Zoë. Have you had a good time?'

'I wish I didn't have to go back really, Phineas.' She held up her hands in resignation. 'I know. I know I don't belong here. It's just that they accept me here, not like at my new school.'

'You seem a lot happier than when I first met you, Zoë. You came into my shop looking lost and lonely.'

'I was, Phineas. I feel like I've grown up now though. I think helping with your problem here has made me a stronger person.'

Roseena gave Zoë a hug.

'We will always be in your debt, Zoë. Although the mermaids didn't hurt me, it was frightening, being taken away and held for ransom.'

Phineas stood up. 'Right Zoë, let's go. Roseena are you coming with us?'

Roseena looked across at Indi and Ruby, who were organising a game of volleyball.

'Do you mind if I don't, Zoë?'

'No, you go and join your friends, thanks for a lovely time.'

Zoë had a strange feeling, she couldn't quite understand why.

Conclusion

Zoë worked harder at school because she wanted to do well.

It was nearly the end of term and Zoë received her school report. She took it home and gave it to her mother.

'Well done, Zoë. What lovely comments from your teachers. It looks like you've improved your grades in every subject.

Her visits to Serendipity had opened her eyes and she saw everything around her in a different light.

'I've made some new friends too, Mum. When I see someone sitting alone, I remember how lonely I was when I started at the school, so I know what it feels like to be left out.'

'Your teacher says here that your classmates have chosen you to represent them on the school council.'

'Yes. Do you remember how I couldn't make friends at first. What a difference now.

Oh, and I've been invited to a barbecue on Friday a birthday party.'

'That's nice for you.'

Zoë still considered herself privileged, having her visits to Serendipity. She never disclosed anything about Phineas, Roseena or her other friends to anyone.

'Where have you suddenly found this new confidence from, Zoë?'

Zoë just shrugged. 'I don't know what you mean.'

'You've grown up in the last couple of months, Zoë. I'm really proud of you.'

★

The next time Zoë went to 'Another Dimension' she was just about to push open the door when someone tapped her on the shoulder. She jumped. She hadn't seen anyone near the shop as she'd approached. When she saw who it was, she froze.

'What do you want?'

It was the old woman who Zoë hated for being so sly.

'Just wanted to say: It's over. The merfolk have left. Tell the old man, will you?'

Then the woman disappeared, not waiting

for a reply from Zoë.

Zoë entered the shop. Phineas was sitting in the back, two mugs of tea already on the table in front of him.

'Message for you, Phineas: from that wicked woman. She was outside just now. It's over. The merfolk have gone.'

'Oh…that's good.' Then it went quiet and Zoë felt uncomfortable.

'Sit down Zoë.'

His serious tone alarmed Zoë. 'What's wrong, Phineas?'

'I didn't want to spoil our lovely day, last time I saw you.'

'I hear a 'but' coming.' Zoë picked up her mug.

'I've sold the grandfather clock.'

She couldn't believe it.

'Zoë, it's time,' he said softly, taking her hand. 'There are others who need to use it.'

'I know, Phineas, but I'll miss everyone so much. Does that mean you're leaving too?'

'Yes, Zoë. The shop is closing.'

He gave Zoë a musical jewellery box. It was made from a reddish wood, covered with seashells, mother of pearl and quartz crystals.

'If ever you need me, wind up the box. The tunes are my flute playing. It will remind you that I am not far away, just in a different dimension.'

Zoë opened the box. Inside was the golden comb and mirror. 'I can't take these, Phineas, they're far too valuable.'

'Yes you can, Zoë. Remember what happened to Roseena. We can never repay you for what you did to keep the secret of the end of the rainbow.'

Tears rolled down Zoë's cheeks. Phineas took a multi-coloured handkerchief from his coat pocket and wiped the tears away.

'Don't cry, Zoë. Look what Serendipity has given you. Apart from new friends and an adventure you'll never forget. You're now a happier, more confident individual.'

Zoë hugged Phineas tightly.

'I'll never forget you, Phineas.'

He tucked the coloured handkerchief into her hand. 'Roseena and I will always remember you Zoë. Bless you.'

I wonder who will enter the grandfather clock next?

THE END